First published by Parragon in 2013

Parragon
Chartist House
15–17 Trim Street
Bath BA1 1HA, UK
www.parragon.com

Written by Catherine Hapka
Illustrated by Grace Lee

ISBN 978-1-4723-3053-6

Printed in China

Disney
Sofia
the First

Written by
Catherine Hapka

Illustrated by
Grace Lee

PaRragon

Bath • New York • Singapore • Hong Kong • Cologne • Delhi
Melbourne • Amsterdam • Johannesburg • Shenzhen

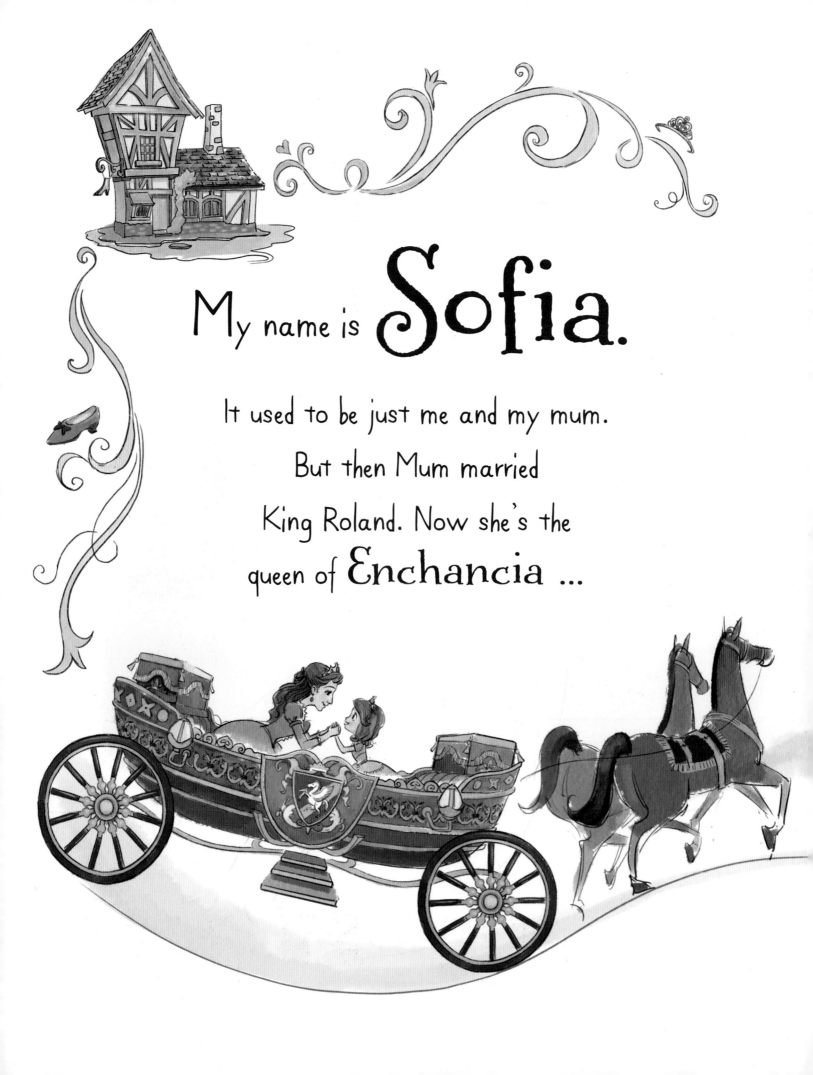

My name is Sofia.

It used to be just me and my mum.
But then Mum married
King Roland. Now she's the
queen of Enchancia ...

... and I'm a
princess!

The trouble is, I don't really know anything
about being a **princess**.

I've never had to do a
royal wave ...

... I'm not sure when
to curtsy ...

... or even which fork
to use at dinner.

I'll never be as perfect a **princess** as my new stepsister, Amber.

"Just be yourself and you'll be fine,"
Mum tells me.

I'm not sure that will work. How can I be **myself** and be a **princess** at the same time?

Then King Roland – um,
I mean my new dad – tries to help.
He gives me a beautiful necklace
called the

Amulet of Avalor

Dad says it's a welcome-to-the-family gift
and that lots of **princesses** before me
have worn it.

Then he tells me we're having a royal ball in my honour. He says we'll dance the first waltz together. That's another thing I don't know how to do - dance!

Maybe there will be a dance class at my new school, Royal Prep Academy. The headmistresses are three fairies named

Flora,

Fauna and

Merryweather.

They promise to
teach me everything
about being a
princess.

Hooray! I do have a dance class! Amber lends me a
pair of special shoes. I think she's starting to like me.

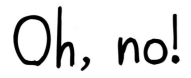

Oh, no!

Amber tricked me!
These shoes are under
a **magic** spell.

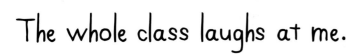

The whole class laughs at me.

But even worse,
I still don't know
how to waltz,
and

the

ball

is

tonight!

Then I remember Cedric, the sorcerer at the castle. James, my stepbrother, says he has all sorts of **magic** spells.

I ask Cedric to help. He writes down some **magic** words. He says if I read them out at the ball, I'll be able to waltz like a real **princess.**

"All hail Princess Sofia!" says Baileywick as I enter the ballroom.

"Shall we dance?" the king asks.

I read out Cedric's **magic** words.

Somnibus

But I don't start to dance.

Populis Cella!

Instead, everyone at the ball falls asleep – even Cedric!

Oh, no!

What have I done? "Help!" I cry.

Suddenly,

my amulet
glows

and

Cinderella appears!

"Your amulet brought me here," she tells me. "When a **princess** is in trouble, another will come to help."

"Can you undo the spell, Cinderella?"
"No, I can't, but your new sister might be able to help."

"But Amber's been so mean to me!" I say.

Cinderella knows what it's like to
have mean stepsisters.
"I wish I had given my stepsisters
a second chance," she says.
"Perhaps that's what Amber needs."

Then she **disappears**.

Amber is still in her room. She never
made it to the ball. She finally tells me
why she's been acting so mean.

"I was worried that everyone would like
you more than me," she says sadly.

"No one could ever be as perfect a
princess as you, Amber!"

I tell her about Cedric's **magic** spell. We search his workshop ...

and find a spell that will wake everyone up.

We hurry to the ballroom.

"Wait," Amber says. "I owe you a dance lesson."

Now I know we're true sisters - and **ever-after friends.**

When I get to the ballroom, I say the
magic words and everyone wakes up.
Then the king and I begin to waltz.

I look over at Amber and smile.
I can't believe how happy I am!
I think I'm going to fit into this
royal family after all.

"Sofia," my dad says, "I'm so proud of you. You dance wonderfully!"

"Thank you, Your Majesty – I mean, Dad."

"You know, Sofia, being a princess is about having a good heart. And you're going to make a great **princess**."

"Dad, I've been wondering ...
why do they call you King Roland the Second?"

"Because my father was also named Roland."

"Well ..." I say, "I guess that makes me

Sofia the First!"

And I am one princess who can't wait to see what happens tomorrow and all the days happily ever after!

The End